LADYBIRD BOOKS

UK | USA | Canada | Ireland | Australia | India | New Zealand | South Africa

Ladybird Books is part of the Penguin Random House group of companies
whose addresses can be found at global.penguinrandomhouse.com.

www.penguin.co.uk   www.puffin.co.uk   www.ladybird.co.uk

Penguin
Random House
UK

First published 2021
001

Adapted by Rebecca Gerlings

Printed in China

The authorized representative in the EEA is Penguin Random House Ireland,
Morrison Chambers, 32 Nassau Street, Dublin D02 YH68

A CIP catalogue record for this book is available from the British Library

ISBN: 978-0-241-48679-5

All correspondence to:
Ladybird Books, Penguin Random House Children's
One Embassy Gardens, 8 Viaduct Gardens, London SW11 7BW

BLUEY

GOODNIGHT FRUIT BAT

Bluey, Bingo, Mum and Dad are playing Pop-Up Croc.
"Again!" cries Bluey when the game ends.
"No, that's it. Bedtime," replies Mum.

Not fair. Bluey doesn't want to go to bed.

"All right," says Dad, following Bluey and Bingo outside.
"Say goodnight to the animals."
Bingo waves. "Night, kangaroos. Night, bilbies."
"Night, fruit bats," says Dad.
"No, fruit bats don't sleep at night. They're 'octurnal,'"
explains Bingo.

"You mean they don't need to
go to bed now?" gasps Bluey.
"No, but you do," says Dad.

Bluey wishes she were a fruit bat.

"But fruit bats don't get to play 'Rocket Ship'!" says Dad.
Bluey and Bingo strap in, and Dad zooms them upstairs
to the bathroom.

"I don't need a shower," complains Bluey.
"Yeah, you do, ya grub," says Dad.

"Not fair. I bet **fruit bats** don't
need to have showers," says Bluey.

But fruit bats don't get to play "Penguins"!
Bluey slides along the wet bathroom floor.
"Look at me, Mum!" she shouts.

WHEEEEEEEEEE!

"Oh, wackadoo!" Mum laughs.
"Teeth time."

Bluey and Bingo brush their teeth and go to the toilet, but Bluey
still isn't tired.

"Not fair," she says. "I wanna stay up like the fruit bats."

"When fruit bats go to the toilet, they hang upside down so their
wee runs all over them!" says Dad.

"Urgh!" cries Bingo.

"I'd *love* that!" says Bluey, giggling.

"I bet you would, you little grub," says Dad.

"I just wanna be a **fruit bat**," says Bluey.
"But fruit bats don't get to play the story game!" says Dad.

Dad starts reading. "The little puppy opened the door, but out jumped a huge . . . hairy . . ."

SNORE!

"Wake up!" the kids squeal.
"... spider!" Dad yells.
They laugh until Mum comes in
and kisses them goodnight.

Not fair. Bluey wants to be a fruit bat, not to go to bed.

Bluey sneaks downstairs and cheekily asks Mum if she can stay up.

Dad is asleep on the floor, dreaming about playing touch footy.
"He doesn't get to play much anymore," Mum explains.

"Why doesn't he get to play it for real life?" asks Bluey.
"He's busy, sweetheart, working and looking after you two," says Mum.
That doesn't seem very fair.

Bluey has an idea.

If Dad dreams about footy, maybe she can dream about being a **fruit bat**. She runs back up to bed.

Bluey closes her eyes, and all of a sudden she's soaring high above their house, flapping her arms like a **fruit bat**.

She flies past bedroom windows
and sees Mackenzie fast asleep.

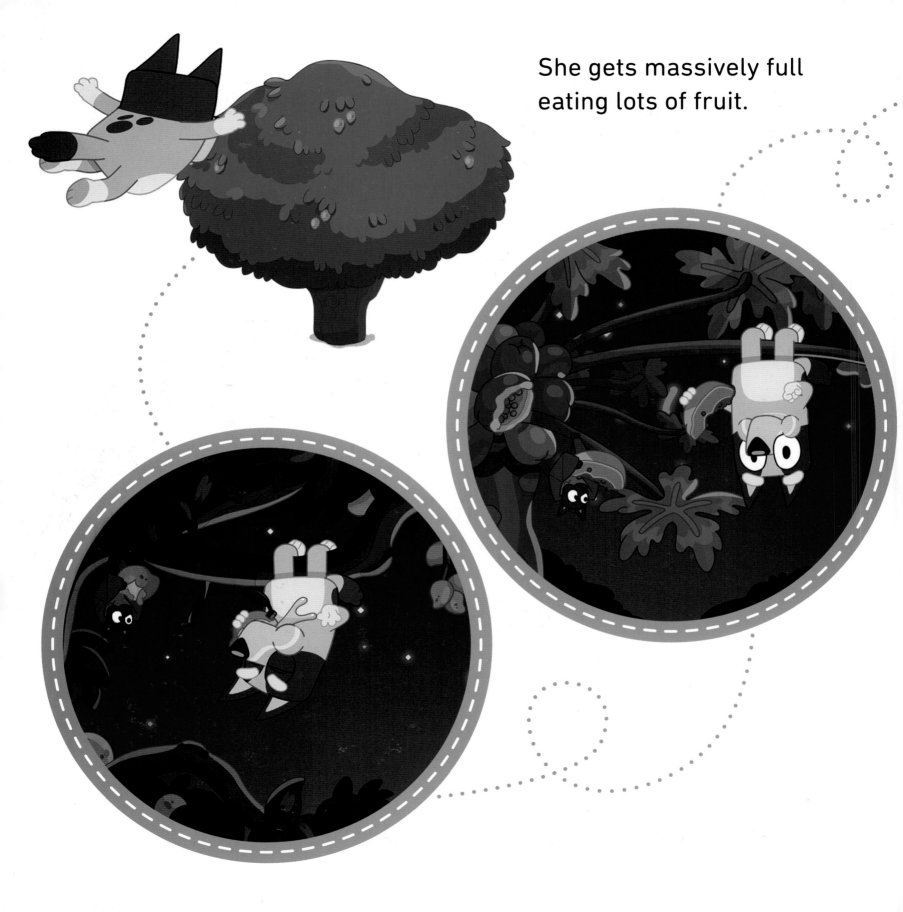

She gets massively full
eating lots of fruit.

BUUUUUURRRP!

Then, Bluey hears a familiar voice in the distance . . .

It's Dad playing footy with his friends.

"Hey, Dad!" yells Bluey, waving.
"Hey, Bluey! You're a fruit bat!"
says Dad. "How is it?"
"It's great," says Bluey. "You get to
eat a lot of fruit."

It looks like Dad is having a lot of fun playing footy. No wonder he misses it.

It's time to head home.

When Bluey wakes up the next morning,
she thinks about Dad. It doesn't seem fair
that he doesn't get to play footy for real life.

But she's never heard him
whinge about it. Not even once.

"I had the most amazing dream," Bluey says, walking into the kitchen for breakfast.
Dad's doing sit-ups, so he's ready for when he plays footy again one day. Bluey has something to tell him . . .

"One, two, three, four . . ." he counts,
lifting her up and down.

"Thanks for looking after us, Dad,"
Bluey says, giving him a hug.
"You're welcome."